Curious George®

GOES TO A TOY STORE

Adapted from the Curious George film series

Edited by Margret Rey and Alan J. Shalleck

SCHOLASTIC INC.
New York Toronto London Auckland Sydney

ISBN 0-590-45292-4

12 11 10 9 8 7 6 5 4 3 2 1   1 2 3 4 5 6/9

Printed in the U.S.A.   24

First Scholastic printing, November 1991

"There's a new toy store opening today,
George," said his friend.
"Let's go downtown and see it."

When they arrived they saw a big crowd
waiting outside.

"I'm going to park the car," said the man
with the yellow hat. "Wait here
and don't get into trouble, George."

George ran to the front of the line.

He ran right past the surprised owner,
who had just opened the door.

There was so much to see inside . . .
dolls, bicycles, and games.

George tried to pull down a hoop
to play with. He pulled and pulled.

The whole pile came tumbling down.
Hoops rolled everywhere.

George picked one up and tried to Hula Hoop.

Everyone laughed and pointed at him.

Then George pretended to be a wheel.
He rolled and rolled —

– right into the owner!

"You're making a mess of my new store!"
the owner shouted, and tried to grab George.

George jumped up to the highest shelf to get
away. "Hey, look up there!"
shouted a little boy. "It's George."

"Mom, can he get me that doll with the pink
dress that you couldn't reach?" asked a girl.

George picked up the doll
and tossed it to the girl.

"Can you reach that game for me, George?"
asked another boy.

George reached up, grabbed the game,
and threw it to the boy.

"Thanks a lot, George," he said.

"Mom, can I get that puppet over there?"
asked a girl.

How good that George was a monkey!
He jumped off the shelf, hung onto a light,
and got the puppet for the girl.

The kids laughed and cheered!
"Great show, George!" they shouted.

"What's going on here?" asked the owner.
He was angry.

"It's George!" said a boy.
"Having him work for you is a great idea."

The owner looked up.
"Well, I guess it is a good idea," he said.

George's friend came over to see what was
going on. "It's time to go now, George.
That's enough monkey business for one day."

"But monkey business is the best business,"
said the owner.

George came down from the shelf.

"Thank you, George, for making my grand
opening such a success," said the
owner. "And here's a surprise for you."

George and his friend waved good-bye
and headed for home.